DARCY MOON
and the
AROONA
FROGS

by
CATHERINE CARVELL

illustrated by
MICHAEL SCOTT PARKINSON

STAR BRIGHT BOOKS
CAMBRIDGE MASSACHUSETTS

Published by Star Bright Books in the United States of America in 2016.

Text copyright © 2014 Catherine Carvell
Illustrations copyright © 2014 Michael Scott Parkinson
First published as "Darcy Moon and the Deep Fried Fogs" by Fremantle Press,
Australia in 2014.

The name Star Bright Books and the Star Bright Books logo are registered
trademarks of Star Bright Books, Inc. Please visit: www.starbrightbooks.com.
For bulk orders, please email: orders@starbrightbooks.com, or call customer
service at: (617) 354-1300.

Printed on paper from sustainable forests.

Paperback ISBN-13: 978-1-59572-752-7
Star Bright Books / MA / 00106160
Printed in Canada / Marquis / 9 8 7 6 5 4 3 2 1

Library of Congress Cataloging-in-Publication Data is available.

To Jeff,
for your support and encouragement,
each step of the way.

TOTALLY EMBARRASSING

Mom had her bum in the air, Dad was crawling about in the mud, and I couldn't stand it anymore.

"How did I end up with such crazy parents?" I groaned, rolling my eyes in frustration. "No other girl in fourth grade has to live with embarrassing weirdos. Why me?"

Mom moved out of her Downward Dog yoga pose, balanced herself on one leg, and pressed her palms above her head. Her armpit hairs fluttered in the breeze.

"Ohmmmmm . . ." she said.

"Why can't we use a lighter like normal people?" I said, striking the flint for the hundredth time and failing to get a spark — again!

"A flint is gentler on the ozone, Darcy," said Dad, gently tugging an earthworm from the dirt with his fingers. It kicked and squirmed in the palm of his hand.

"Can you eat ozone?" I said. "Because we'll starve before I get this fire going."

"The trick is sock fluff," said Dad. "Sock fluff always gets a spark. But if you can't wait for the lentil burgers, there's plenty of mung-bean salad and gluten-free bread in the cooler."

"Ohmmmmm . . . " said Mom.

Things couldn't get any worse. Or so I thought, until a car pulled into the park, and squinting through its back window was Michael, a kid from my class. If he looked over now, I'd be

a living joke before I could say *Not related to me.*
I quickly crouched behind the barbecue, messed
my hair over my face, and looked about for a
place to hide.

The earthy whiff of the wetland wafted past
my nostrils. Of course!

"I'm going to check out the swamp,"
I said, scurrying past Dad. I pushed through the
reeds, slipped down the bank, and slopped into
ankle-deep mud. Turning around, I shimmied
back up the slope, just far enough to look out from
behind a paperbark tree trunk.

Dad's eyes were wide with delight. "Off she
goes exploring the natural world," he said.

Mom was doing a happy dance. "She's so
in tune!" she cried, waving her hands in the air.
"Whoop, whoop, whoop!"

It was awful.

But my super-quick thinking had worked.
Michael hadn't seen me. I almost broke into

my own little happy dance but was all of a sudden distracted. A cold, slimy wetness seeped into my socks, and a raspy gulp echoed from the mud puddles behind me. "Holy croak! It's Darcy Moon!"

HOLY CROAK

"Well, don't just stand there like a stunned slug. Get a wiggle on!" The voice seemed to come from a large green frog. It glared at me from a patch of pondweed.

"Er, excuse me?" I stammered, looking around for someone — anyone — hiding in the rushes.

"Holy croak, girl, we don't have time for this." The voice was definitely coming from the frog. "My family's been missing all night. They could be barbecued frogs' legs by now!"

I squeezed my eyes shut and opened them again. Was I hallucinating? Or was someone playing a trick? Someone who knew my name?

I looked around for a hidden camera.
I couldn't see one but tried to look cool anyway,
just in case I was being recorded. Casually
strolling forward, I lunged suddenly and grabbed
the frog. It was slippery and cold and I could feel
a tiny heart beating against my palm. Letting out
a scream, I tossed it away. It landed in a writhing
green heap in the mud.

"What are you doing?" the frog shouted
at me. "Don't you get it?" Bits of slime and spit
were squirting out of his mouth. "We are in a
HURRY!" His croak was more of a manic squeal
by now, and his throat sac pumped faster than a
cicada's back leg at dusk.

"I don't understand," I said.

A scaly brown tortoise ambled from behind a
blackened log. "Allow me to explain," it said.

"What the . . . ?" I said, sitting down heavily.
"Who the . . . ?"

"My name is Wizen," said the tortoise. "I am called Wizen because I am wise and somewhat wizened."

"O-kaaay," I said. But things were definitely NOT okay.

"This is Jumpy," said Wizen, turning his solemn gray eyes in the direction of the talking frog. "He is called Jumpy because he is nervous by nature and jumps a lot."

"Makes sense," I said. But it absolutely did NOT make sense.

Wizen nodded his wrinkled head and carried on. "Many of the swamp frogs have been going missing. It started about a year ago. Just a few at first, then more and more until now we can wait no longer. We need your help."

"You said she had mystical powers," interrupted Jumpy, squirming himself out of the mud. He glared at Wizen. "But she's slower than Old Granny Snail with a blister on her foot. Tell her we need to GO!"

"Jumpy is feeling particularly nervous today," said Wizen, scrumphing about in the mud. "I know you are anxious, Jumpy," he said, "but you need to have patience . . . Darcy Moon is perplexed."

"Yes." I said, nodding. "I am perplexed. And how do you know my name?"

"The Universe has chosen you as an Earth Guardian," said Wizen, calmly pushing his knobbled neck out from his shell. "She chose you to save the frogs. Like she chose Jacques Cousteau to save the oceans. Like she chose Steve Irwin to save the crocodiles."

"Um," I said, "aren't those guys both dead?"

"The night you were born," he said, ignoring my question, "there was a rare lunar eclipse. The planets were aligned." He lifted a webbed foot and waved it in the air as if the planets were hovering in front of him. "When the eclipse passed," he continued, "the first ray of moonlight hit your newborn eyes, and a cosmic dose of planetary magic passed to you."

"But I'm just a normal kid," I protested.

"Earth Guardian powers can lie dormant for many years, stirred only by the callings of an animal in need." His neck trembled with the strain of holding up his ancient, weather-beaten head. "The animals need you now."

"This is an EMERGENCY!!!" yelled Jumpy, jumping up and down. "We need you right now!"

I gaped at the crazy scene before me. "I'm getting out of here," I said.

"You alone can help us," announced Wizen. "We will wait for your return."

"Don't bother," I muttered as I scrambled up the bank. I mean, life was weird enough already with my parents around. I certainly didn't need a freaked-out frog and a spooky old tortoise on my back as well.

PILE OF POO

"Darcy!" cried Mom when she saw me trudging toward her. "You look like a half-starved swamp monster."

"Want a burger?" Dad dangled a crusty old sock in my face. "I got a great fire started with your flint," he said. "All it needed was a bit of sock fluff, and *kaboom!*"

I screwed up my nose. "I'm not hungry. I want to go home."

"Already?" asked Dad, looking surprised. Then he shrugged. "Okay. I've got all the wigglers I need for today." We packed the leftovers into the cooler and headed for home.

Mom and Dad didn't believe in cars. They said exhaust fumes were choking the Earth and

melting the icebergs. We walked everywhere …
or rode our bikes. Sometimes I wished we had
a car, but right then I was too stunned to think
about it much. We traipsed the ten minutes across
the grassland and down the bush track to the hole
in our back fence.

I went through the hole first, closely followed
by the cooler and then Mom. She frowned at me.
"You look pale," she said. "I'll burn some cypress
and lemon oils to get your blood flowing."

Dad squeezed through last and gazed
lovingly up at our compost pile. "Don't get
yourselves all tied up in knots," he said, emptying
his slimy collection of worms into a heap on the
dirt. "I have brought you to worm heaven," he
said. "Be free, little wigglers."

We made our way around the compost heap,
which wasn't easy because it filled our backyard
right to the edges. We had to turn sideways and
shimmy along the fence single file.

I would've preferred a regular yard like other kids. You know, one that didn't steam in the heat or look like giant mounds of damp vegetation. But Dad made compost for a living. Our backyard is worm heaven, but it is definitely not a place I could hang out with my friends.

When we finally got inside, I was about to go straight to my room but paused. "Mom," I asked, "what was my birth like?"

Mom beamed. "Oh Darcy, it was the most spiritual moment of my life! We were in the garden — the compost pile wasn't as big then. It was the night of an eclipse. I wanted to see you as soon as you were born, but it was too dark. Your father had just decided to light candles when, like a miracle, the shadow passed and you were born into moonlight." She smiled and sighed. "You were so beautiful," she cooed. "My darling baby girl. You were naked, and I was naked, and your father was nak — "

"Okay, Mom," I said and closed my bedroom door with a bang.

THE COOL CROWD

As I rode my bike to school — Quagmire
Primary — the next day, I tried to convince
myself nothing had changed. I mean, I still knew
how to pull an awesome dust-cloud skid at the
bottom of our driveway, sprint the ring road
around Aroona Park, speed past the rows of
broccoli on Market Garden Road, and reach the
outskirts of sleepy Quagmire town in less than
fifteen minutes. Yep. Everything was the same
as usual. So, as I cruised by Quagmire's statue
of a giant cabbage, I tried not to think about
disappearing frogs and talking swamp creatures.
But it was hard going. How could you put

something like that out of your mind? I wanted to talk to someone about it. But it sounded crazy even to me. So I didn't tell anyone. Not even my best friend, Jedda.

"G'day, Darce!" yelled Jedda, waving at me from the water fountains. "How was the rest of your weekend?"

"Boring," I called as I spun the combination on my bike lock. I headed over to our usual spot under the peppermint tree. "Aroona Park with my crazy parents." Flopping down on the grass, we rummaged around in our bags for food.

Jedda found a Vegemite sandwich and took a bite. "Did you see my dad there?" she asked with her mouth full. "He was doing nature talks."

I shook my head. "No. But I saw Michael."

Jedda's eyebrows scrunched together like a couple of grumbling caterpillars. "You didn't hide, did you?"

"Of course I did. I was with my parents."

I pried the lid off my lunch box. "GROSS! Leftover lentil burgers." I shoved the squishy globs under Jedda's nose as evidence. "See what I mean? My parents are so not normal."

Jedda wrinkled up her nose. "Get a grip, Darcy," she said. "Your mom and dad are really nice. And anyway, who cares what other people think?"

"I do," I said, staring through my tangled hair at my disgusting lunch. I clicked the lid back on. "I'll take this home for the worms."

"Here comes Taylor," said Jedda, nodding in the direction of the water fountains. Taylor always said hi to us in the mornings, which was good of her because she was really popular, and in case you hadn't guessed, Jedda and I weren't. We had each other and that was enough. But everybody loved Taylor.

"Hi, guys. How are you?" she piped. Her friends crowded round her like moths to a flame.

Sometimes I wished I could be the flame for once. "Anything good, Darcy?" she said, eyeing my lunch box.

"Just leftovers."

"Want to come to the canteen with us? Skippity Chips have finally reached Quagmire. We're all getting some."

Jedda frowned. "We don't have any mon — "

I jabbed her in the ribs with my elbow. "Sure!" I exclaimed. I jumped to my feet and pulled Jedda up by her T-shirt. "I've got cash," I whispered.

Jedda pulled herself free of my grip and glared at me.

"Come on, Jedda," I begged. "Please?" I grabbed her arm and started walking toward the canteen.

"Where did you get cash?" said Jedda.

"Save-a-Species fundraiser," I explained.

"You're going to use your donation money

to buy Skippity Chips? Darcy Moon, won't your mom chuck a complete wobbly?" Jedda had to shout over all the excited chatter and rustling chip bags as we entered the canteen.

"She won't find out." I narrowed my eyes and fixed Jedda with the most intense stare I could manage.

"Whatever." She shrugged. "As long as you buy me a bag too." She gave a mischievous grin. "Have you seen the ad yet?"

I rolled my eyes. "How could I when we don't have a television?"

I hadn't seen the Skippity Chips ad, but I had seen an article in the local newspaper about the guy who invented them. I was amazed because he went to Quagmire Primary too, except thirty years ago. And now he was a millionaire!

I finally got to the counter and ordered two bags. I felt pretty guilty handing over all the donation money. But I didn't want to miss out.

It had taken a whole year for Skippity Chips to arrive in Quagmire shops. And besides, I was starving.

I gave Jedda her bag, and we ripped them open together.

They looked like regular potato chips. Round and flat except for where they'd curled and bubbled in the hot oil. I put one in my mouth and sucked off the powdery flavoring. It bubbled and popped on my tongue like a savory fizz bomb.

"Yum!" said Jedda. "There's a party in my mouth!"

I swallowed the first chip down and grabbed another handful. This time I chewed them all up and swished them around my mouth before swallowing. Delicious!

Finally tipping the crumbs at the bottom of the bag into my mouth, I looked around at all the other kids chatting and smiling and licking their lips. For a minute it actually looked like Jedda and

I were part of the cool crowd.

"What flavor do you think they are?"
I asked, sucking the spicy green salt off my fingers.

Jedda checked the label. "It just says natural
flavors on the bag."

"Taste like chicken kebabs with garlic sauce
to me," said Taylor.

"Sour cream and onion?" I suggested.

"Whatever it is," said Jedda, "they're
delicious!"

Just then I heard
the clanking of the
donation can.

"Save-a-Species!
Donation money this
way!" called Michael
as he made his way
through the crowd.

Taylor wiped
her hands on a pink

handkerchief. "Here's my money," she said, dropping her coins into the can. The other kids grappled through their pockets.

I kept my head down, gazed into my empty chip bag, and hoped Michael wouldn't notice me. But he stopped right in front of me and shook the can in my face.

"Cough up, Mooney," he commanded.

I felt a hot lump in my chest. I wasn't sure if it was guilt or indigestion, but whatever it was, I wished I hadn't eaten those chips.

"Um … I don't have any money," I mumbled.

"What?" shouted Michael. "No Money Mooney!"

Michael's friends snorted. The other kids sniggered, and even Taylor had a quiet giggle.

Jedda didn't laugh. She just looked at me and shrugged. "Come on," she said, "let's go." We threw our chip wrappers in the garbage can and walked to class.

"Now see why I hid at the park yesterday?" I said. "My whole life is one big embarrassment after another."

As we clattered into the classroom, Jedda gave me a pitying look. Sitting down, she pulled her writing pads and pencils out of her bag. "You worry too much," she said, arranging them on her desk.

You'd worry too, I thought, if you had the world's biggest hippies for parents. But another thought wasn't going away, and it made having kooky parents seem kind of unimportant. Kids catching sight of my mom's hairy armpits would be bad, but kids finding out I talked to frogs and tortoises would be really, really, *really* bad!

ENDANGERED

I had trouble concentrating in class.

In math I doodled a dozen trapezoid turtles and a very cute polygon frog.

In English I daydreamed about a school of tadpoles doing spelling tests, eager for a smiley stamp from their teacher, Mr. Tortoise.

Then we had science.

"Last week we looked at ecosystems," said Mr. Bainbridge. "We discovered all animals are linked via the food chain. We saw how small changes in habitat can have devastating effects on native animals. Who can remember some of the endangered species we looked at last week?"

Taylor's arm shot up. "The cassowary and the quoll from the Daintree Rainforest."

"Excellent, Taylor. Anyone else?"

"The *bum*-dicoot," sniggered Michael under his breath.

"The *bum*-bat," snickered his friend with a muffled snort.

Mr. Bainbridge sighed. "The *ban*dicoot and the *num*bat," he said, looking directly at the boys, "are indeed close to extinction. Which is no laughing matter. But today we will look closer to home. Does anyone know of an endangered animal that lives right here in Quagmire?"

There was silence apart from a chair leg scraping on the linoleum and the swooshing of a sprinkler outside the window.

"Anyone?"

"My dad works at Aroona Park," said Jedda. "He says Western Swamp Tortoises are endangered."

"He's right, Jedda," said Mr. Bainbridge, unrolling a poster and pinning it onto the display board. "This," he announced, "is Quagmire's very own endangered species."

I felt my face turn grayer than a Western Swamp Tortoise's toenail, and suddenly I couldn't concentrate hard enough.

I was looking at a picture of Wizen.

"They were thought to be extinct," said Mr. Bainbridge, "but in 1954 a schoolkid, just like you, took one to a wildlife show. A breeding program was started at Perth Zoo, and since then, a few of these beautiful tortoises have been rereleased at Aroona Park," he said. "The money raised through our Save-a-Species fundraiser will be donated to Aroona … to conserve the tortoises' habitat."

I felt greener than a queasy frog's throat sac.

An endangered species had asked me for help. And I'd run away.

SWAMP SICKNESS

That night I couldn't sleep, so I pulled out my split ends and arranged them in a row on my pillow. I kept going until I had a headache. I didn't want to be an Earth Guardian. I didn't want to talk to animals. But I was pulling my hair out! I had no choice. I had to go back to the swamp.

I grabbed my backpack and looked around my room. What would I need for a midnight frog search expedition? I gathered my flashlight, binoculars, a bottle of water, my fire-starting flint, and the Swiss Army knife Dad gave me for my birthday last year. After pulling on sneakers,

I grabbed some extra socks from my drawer. One thing was for certain: it was sure to get sloppy down there in the swamp.

I crept out of the house, past the compost heap, and through the hole in the back fence. My feet crunched on the gravel as I walked. The silence of the night seemed to be everywhere, broken only by the far-off rumble of traffic and the shrill clicking of a hidden cicada. The moon was full and gave me enough light to see the way. But there were dark places and spaces behind every bush. And everything had a spooky moonlit glow. When I got to the swamp, I slipped down the bank into the water, sending ripples circling out from my feet. The full moon reflecting on the surface swayed gently, like an old yellow sloth in a dark and liquid sky.

I pushed through the shallows and smacked into a swarm of mosquitoes. They zipped about in a feeding frenzy, buzzing in my ears and biting my skin. I slapped my neck and wiped the mess on my jeans before swatting another one off my nose.

"Holy croak! You came back!" cried Jumpy, tearing a frenzied path toward me through the duckweed.

"I couldn't stay away," I said.

Jumpy's back legs whirred hysterically as he leaped toward me and fell at my feet in a panic-stricken plop. "Things are really urgent now," he said. "I'm the only frog left." He let out a long mournful wail, then snapped out his tongue and pulled a crowd of shrieking mosquitoes into his slimy throat.

"At least you have plenty of lunch," hissed a weary-looking tiger snake. "I'm ssstarving and weak as a worm without my froggy sssnacks."

Jumpy gave a nervous hop, and I quickly positioned myself in between the two of them.

"No need to get jumpy, Jumpy," said the

snake. "I know you're the lassst frog ssstanding. If I eat you, I'll have no chance of tasssting frog again." Then he opened his cavernous mouth and let out a rancid burp.

My stomach churned, and Jumpy slapped two webbed fingers over his nose holes. His eyes filled with tears. "That's disgusting!" he retched.

"It is egg you can smell." Wizen inched his stubby legs toward us from behind a clump of bulrushes. "Tortoise egg." He looked a shade grayer than the last time I saw him. And older too.

"No hard feelingsss, old chap," said the snake. "I'd prefer a frog to a tortoise egg any day. But there are no more frogsss. It's a culinary catassstrophe!" And with that he slithered across a wet stone and disappeared into the undergrowth.

"Things are not good," said Wizen, nodding slowly and blinking his tiny gray eyes. "The food chain is broken. The wetland is dying." He hung his head in the mud. "It is a relief you have returned."

"I'm sorry I didn't come back earlier," I said, a horrible sense of dread settling into my stomach. Were the frogs gone forever? Would the tortoises die out? Would the wetland survive? "I really want to help," I whispered. And I meant it.

Jumpy opened his mouth to speak. Half-munched mosquitoes sprayed out in all directions, but before he could say anything, there was a sudden movement from the other side of the wetland.

I dropped to my knees, scrambled to the cover of a nearby paperbark tree, and peered into the shadows.

FROGNAPPED

There, standing knee-deep in the swamp water, swearing loudly and swatting at a swarm of mosquitoes, was a dodgy-looking man in gumboots and wading overalls. His oily hair was slicked to the side and a pointy nose poked out between two puffy cheeks. His stomach made a tight bulge around his middle, and I couldn't help thinking he looked like an angry, overweight penguin.

"I've seen him here before," gulped Jumpy. "I thought he was fishing."

"Fishing's illegal," I whispered. "This is a protected wetland."

"For the love of money, get off me!"

The man flapped his arms at the army of mosquitoes that bounced off his chubby cheeks. "I'll teach you to mess with Sid Bellows!" he yelled. "I'll fumigate the lot of you."

Sid Bellows? The name sounded familiar. Come to think of it, his face looked familiar too. I tried to think of where I knew him from but I couldn't remember.

"Hmmm . . . suspicious," murmured Wizen as he examined the scene from the roots of the paperbark.

Springing up the tree trunk, Jumpy positioned himself to get a better view. "If he's not fishing, what's he doing?" he said.

"Be quiet and watch!"

Sid Bellows waddled through the sticky mud. His face was as red as a baboon's bottom. Dark wet patches spread across his back and armpits as he fished around in the muddy water below a clump of bulrushes.

Then, with eyes bulging, he grabbed onto something hidden amongst the willowy stalks and heaved backward. "For the love of money!" he puffed. "You bloaters better be worth your weight in slime." And with that, he fell over backward, hauling a muddy wire cage on top of himself.

Inside the cage was a squirming mass of frogs. There must have been at least twenty. They'd been silent under the water, but now their terrified croaks and squeals burst out in a shrill chorus of foreboding and fear. They hurled themselves at the sides of the cage, trying desperately to break free. But they were stuck fast.

"What on earth is he doing?" I whispered. By now Sid had pulled himself out of the mud and was dragging the cage behind him toward the edge of the swamp.

"Holy croak!" said Jumpy, his

throat sac throbbing in turmoil. "They're being frognapped!"

I unzipped the backpack. "Get in," I said. "We'll follow them."

Jumpy hopped in, and I bent down so Wizen could climb in too. But he just blinked at me and shook his head.

"I am needed here," he said, gazing at me with ancient, troubled eyes. "The wetland is depending on you."

I wanted to tell him I knew how important it was to find the frogs. Not just for Jumpy and the others, but for the whole wetland, for the baby tortoises, for the food chain. But I couldn't find the words. Instead, I placed my hand gently on his back. The touch of his bony shell reminded me of my dad's hand. Hard and calloused, but warm and comforting at the same time. Pulling my bag, with Jumpy in it, tightly onto my shoulders, I turned to follow Sid Bellows.

TRAILER TRASH

I crept after Sid as he stumbled through the mud. He cursed and carried on like a crabby cockatoo. If he kept going like this, it would be too easy — all I had to do was follow the noise and stay low.

"What's he doing?" mumbled Jumpy from inside the backpack.

There was a sudden beep from the parking lot, and the lights of a dark pickup truck with a trailer attached to it flashed twice.

"Holy croak!" shrieked Jumpy, poking his head out. "How can we keep up with a truck?"

"Shh," I hissed. I bet Steve Irwin never had

to deal with a talking frog when he was saving crocodiles.

We watched as Sid undid some ropes at the back of the trailer and pulled a tarpaulin back. He placed the cage under the tarp, retied the knot, and walked back to the truck door.

"What are we going to do?" asked Jumpy, moving onto my shoulder and prodding me with his slippery little foot.

"I want to get in that trailer," I said, "but I think it's all tied up." I fished around in my bag for the binoculars and held them up to my eyes. There was enough light from the moon to see, but no matter how much I twiddled the knob, I couldn't focus on anything useful. Then the number plate zoomed into focus.

"SKIPPITY CHIPS," I said.

"SKIPPITY CHIPS?" said Jumpy.

"Yeah . . . Skippity Chips," I said as I refocused the binoculars onto Sid Bellows's overalls. Then I remembered where I'd seen him. The newspaper. "Of course!"

"Of course *what?*" asked Jumpy.

Sid was struggling to pull off his muddy rubber boots. "No time," I said, eyeing off the trailer. "He's preoccupied. It's now or never."

I hurled the binoculars into the bag and ran, reaching the back of the trailer just as the engine rumbled to life. I shoved Jumpy and the backpack into the gap between the tarp and the trailer, then stuck my head in, but the hole was too small for the rest of me. My heart racing, I felt along the edge of the tarp to where it was secured and pulled at the knot. But it was tied in a double. I couldn't get a decent grip.

Black exhaust fumes swirled around my face as Sid revved the engine. My eyes stung and my vision went blurry. Bits of grit stuck to the back of my throat, making me hack and cough.

"What's taking so long?" cried Jumpy over
the roar of the car.

"The knot's too tight."

"Use this!" shouted Jumpy, holding up my
Swiss Army knife.

"Great thinking," I said.
I flicked the blade and sliced the rope. My
shoulders followed easily, but I still couldn't pull
my legs through. Half of me was in. Half of me
was out. And the car had started moving! If
I didn't get my legs off the asphalt soon, they
were in real danger of being left behind. The car
moved faster, and my legs trotted briskly to keep
up. Next thing I knew, I was jogging … then
running … then sprinting. Grappling blindly
with my hands, I managed to grab hold of
something metal and pulled as hard as I could.
Finally my legs slithered through the tarp, and
I fell onto the trailer floor.

"Wow!" said Jumpy. "That was cool."

"Is that you, Jumpy?" came a voice from the frog cage. "It's me, Olive."

"Sis! Are you okay?" The trailer vibrated along the road, juddering and swerving.

"I'm okay," said Olive. "But I've been trapped in this cage all day!"

"Why didn't you croak for help?" asked Jumpy. "I would've found you."

"I did croak. We all did. But every time someone came to help, they got caught too. So we kept quiet." Olive pointed at me with a webbed finger. "Who's she?"

"This is Darcy Moon, the Earth Guardian that Wizen told us about," said Jumpy. Then he lowered his voice and spoke quietly to his sister. "She's a bit slow on the uptake, but she's all we've got."

"Hey!" I protested. "I heard that. At least I've figured out who that guy is. He's Sid Bellows."

"Genius!" said Jumpy, rolling his eyes.

"No, really," I said. "He's famous. He invented Skippity Chips and made heaps of money. He's a big hero."

"Well, if he's such a great guy, why is he throwing imprisoned frogs into a trailer in the dead of night?" asked Jumpy.

The car slowed down, then stopped. "Act natural," I said, and scanned the mess around me, looking for somewhere to hide. I scrambled toward a cardboard box, pulled it over my head, and held my breath. The car door slammed.

I listened as the scrape of footsteps on gravel headed down the side of the trailer. There was a sudden bang as Sid gave the trailer a whack with his fist.

"Come on, you shrieking bags of slime," said Sid, "get those juices flowing. I've got orders to fill." There was a thump and a scrape, then Sid Bellows's footsteps walking away from the trailer.

I slowly peeped out from under the cardboard box and pulled the tarp aside. Darkened tree branches drooped all around me like poisoned stick insects in the night. Eerie puffs of cloud drifted across the sky, casting a ghoulish mist over the moon. Looming to our left was a dingy old warehouse. As I watched, Sid Bellows disappeared inside with the frogs.

"He's got them!" cried Jumpy. "What are we waiting for?"

"I'm scared," I whispered as I gazed at the barbed-wire fence surrounding us.

Jumpy hopped nervously around the edge of the backpack. "Don't back out now, Darcy," he said. "We need you to do this."

I knew he was right, but I felt sick about what might be behind those doors. I didn't want to be here anymore than the frogs did. But at least I had a choice — they didn't.

I climbed out of the trailer, and pushing my mucky hair behind my grimy ears with my grubby fingers, I strode toward the warehouse door.

FROG SCUM

I turned the handle gently and pushed my shoulder against the door. It slowly creaked open, and I peered inside.

Rows and rows of frogs in cages stretched out in front of me like aisles in a supermarket. The electronic hum from blazing lights above and an occasional weak croak were all that broke the oppressive silence. The frogs were haggard and still. Moisture oozed from their skin and dripped into long metallic troughs that ran below them like gutters.

"I think he's collecting frog sweat," I whispered.

"Frogs don't sweat," said Jumpy as he stared at the awful scene before us.

"If they don't sweat, what's that?" I said, pointing to the thick river of swampy frog slime gathering in the troughs.

"Holy croak! It's breathing mucus." His hind legs quivered. "We breathe through our skin. But it has to be moist. If we dry out, we make mucus so we can keep breathing." Jumpy pointed a trembling webbed finger upward. "Look at all those heat lamps," he said. "He's after their slime."

"But why?"

"I have no idea," said Jumpy. "But we have to get these frogs out of here."

"There are so many," I said. I moved Jumpy aside to get to my water bottle. "We need a plan."

I twisted the lid and dribbled water over the back of the frog closest to me.

It glistened for a moment on the skin before being absorbed thirstily away. The frog looked up at me and blinked.

"Are you all right?" I asked gently. "What's happening here?"

"I'LL TELL YOU WHAT'S HAPPENING HERE!" boomed Sid Bellows's voice.

I let out a scream and dropped my bottle, splattering water all over the concrete floor.

"YOU, little girl," he hollered, "are TRESPASSING!"

Jumpy hopped into the backpack, and I turned to see Sid's puffy red face and a bloated finger pointed straight at me. I quickly darted behind a row of cages. "My name is Darcy Moon," I said. "I'm here to save the frogs. Let them go, or I'll report you for animal cruelty!"

"Go home," sneered Sid. "Everything is legal here."

"But these frogs need water," I said. "You can't suffocate them."

Sid smiled, revealing a crooked row of pointy yellow teeth. "You can do anything if you make enough money," he said. "And this," he announced theatrically, throwing his arms out wide, "is a moneymaking machine!"

"As if!" I said. "You can't make money out of frog slime."

"And who made you the expert?" Sid sneered. "Did you spend year after year slogging away in your parents' chip factory? Doing things their way? Never making any money? Wasting all the profits on expensive ingredients? Did you?"

I remembered the newspaper article I'd read about him clearly now. It had said he had taken over the family business when it was about to go bankrupt and managed to turn it into a multimillion-dollar company by releasing the most popular new chip of the century, Skippity Chips — all in less than a year! But what did that have to do with the frogs?

"I'm no expert," I said. "But — "

"No, you are not!" agreed Sid. "It was me who slashed costs. It was me who created the best-tasting chip in the universe. It was my chips that made chip-selling history. My chips! I'm the expert. I'm the millionaire!"

"But I don't get it," I said. "This is a frog-slime factory."

"Yes, it is," said Sid with a pompous wink.

"So what does frog slime have to do with Skippity Chips?"

"Oh, just everything," said Sid as he dipped a pudgy finger into one of the troughs. "Because this frog slop" — he lifted his hand into the air and watched the goopy green liquid drip back into the tray — "is the Skippity Chip secret ingredient!"

ALL NATURAL INGREDIENTS

Stomach gas rushed up my gullet, and a glob of vomit filled my mouth.

Ewww!

I had eaten frog-slime chips.

Ewww!

I swallowed hard and wiped my tongue on my sleeve.

Ewww! Ewww! Ewww!

"That's totally wrong!" I gurgled. "It can't be legal."

"According to my *official* paperwork," said Sid, making quotation marks in the air with his fingers, "Skippity Chips are flavored with local chicken gizzards and imported frog legs. They think this factory is for the chickens, and the frog legs are imported from China — canned and seasoned with garlic," he said. "And it's all there in black-and-white on the packet. *Natural flavors . . . All natural ingredients . . .*" He threw his shiny face into the air and cackled like a half-witted hyena.

This guy was a total nutcase!

"But can't you see you're killing the wetland?"

Sid curled his lip into a smirk. "So what? There's plenty more wetlands when I'm finished with this one."

I really did *not* like Sid Bellows.

"You think you're so great." I grabbed my backpack and ran toward the door. "But you won't feel so hot once I tell everyone the truth!" I shouted over my shoulder.

"Tell them what you want," he scoffed.

"Who are they going to believe? A respectable millionaire or some kooky kid covered in mud?"

I reached the door, but my hand shook so much I couldn't get out. I felt Sid's clammy hand grip my shoulder, and I peered up at his creepy grin.

"I tick all the boxes," he said. "Size of cages, cleanliness, factory fire procedures." He opened the door and shoved me outside. "And just so we are clear," he said, "if you blab" — he pulled a pretend knife across his throat — "I'll kill the lot of them." He slammed the warehouse door between us.

I stood on the asphalt and blinked.
I couldn't believe it. How could clean cages and a fire alarm make it okay to torture frogs?

How could it be okay not telling people that *natural flavors* was actually frog slime?

How could he be getting away with this?

"That guy is one big toad wart!" shrieked

Jumpy as I lifted him out of the packpack. "Now what?"

"I don't know. I need to think."

"Well, you better think quick," said Jumpy. "If those frogs don't get water before sunrise, they'll be more dried out than a slug in a salt bath."

"We'll wait," I said, hiding behind a scrubby wattle bush close to the fence line. I pushed a few prickly branches aside so I had a clear view of the warehouse door. "He has to leave sometime," I said.

"And then what?" asked Jumpy.

"I haven't thought of that yet," I said.

A SLIPPERY RESCUE

We crouched behind the bush so long my
legs went numb. Jumpy fidgeted and gave the
occasional gulp until finally we heard the creak of
the warehouse door.

"This is it," whispered Jumpy. "Ready when
you are!"

I watched as Sid got into his truck and
slowly drove through the gate and down the
road. Waiting until the sound of the engine had
disappeared into the distance, I grabbed the
backpack and scurried through the shadows
to the warehouse. Nervously pushing the door
open, I squinted into the glare of the lights. Were

the frogs still alive? I ran from cage to cage and rattled the doors. The frogs lay silent inside, barely breathing.

"Do something!" demanded Jumpy. He was a very annoying frog in a crisis.

I ignored him and grabbed my Swiss Army knife. I tried cutting the wire with the scissors, but it didn't work. I tried the blade, but that didn't work either. Then I flicked open the screwdriver and stuck it in the keyhole. I twisted and jiggled it. But it was no use.

"Useless!" I hurled the knife back in the backpack.

"We need to get them wet." Jumpy was hopping from cage to cage. "They're running out of time."

I scanned the warehouse. There had to be water somewhere. A tap. A sink. A toilet. Anything. But all I could see were stupid posters of Sid, photos of Sid, cardboard cutouts of Sid

— you name it. The place was done out like some sort of shrine, with every square inch of wall covered with Sid memorabilia. There was a framed photo of Sid shaking hands with the mayor and a whole wall of newspaper cutouts. There was even a floor-to-ceiling poster of Sid in a sports car, grinning at us. Laughing at us.

I felt a trickle of sweat on my forehead and looked up. The sizzling lights beat down on us, scorching like the midday sun. Then I saw the pipes running along the ceiling in rows. That was it!

I pointed upward. "The sprinkler system!" I shouted. "Sid put in sprinklers to pass the fire safety rules."

"Oh, very helpful," said Jumpy. "We'll just sit around and wait for a fire to start, shall we?"

I ran to the wall and ripped down a big poster of Sid. "We can do better than that," I said. I pulled down some newspaper clippings and ripped them into tiny shreds. I fluffed the

paper scraps into a tiny bird's nest, then pulled out my spare socks.

"What are you doing?" squeaked Jumpy.

"Something my dad taught me," I said, picking at the fuzzy round balls of sock lint and sprinkling them over the pile of crumpled paper. I pulled out my flint and struck with the steel striker. Nothing. I struck again and a flicker of sparks skidded across the concrete floor and disappeared. I struck again. Another spark, and this time it hit the sock fluff and burst into an orange glow. I tore the poster into strips and placed pieces on top, being careful not to smother the flame. When I was certain it wouldn't go out, I stood back and watched.

"Whoa!" said Jumpy.

The papers crackled. The smoldering blaze sent a plume of black smoke and tiny flakes of paper ash into the warehouse ceiling. Dad would've been impressed.

I waited for the sprinklers to turn on. But nothing happened. The papers were nearly completely burned away, so I ran to pull more paper off the wall to keep the fire going. And that's when all mayhem broke loose.

First, the earsplitting squeal of a fire alarm pierced the air. Then the sprinklers turned on, and water sprayed all over us like a monsoon rain. The fire fizzed into nothing. The frogs quivered and blinked under the reviving spray. They stretched and hopped on the spot. They croaked excitedly. Then there was an almighty CLANG, and all at once, every cage door in the warehouse flew open.

I couldn't believe it. That was some factory fire response!

"Yahoo!" shouted Jumpy. "You did it!"

Before I knew what was happening, a sea of frogs surrounded me. They hopped and jumped and croaked and gulped and gleamed and dripped with water and relief and the joy of newfound freedom.

"Mom! Dad! Olive! You're alive!" shouted Jumpy and pounced into a very sloppy family hug.

I was happier than a fly caught in a garbage can.

But I couldn't relax just yet.

How was I going to get them all home to the swamp?

HOMEWARD BOUND

I thought back to our journey in the trailer and
guessed it had taken about ten minutes altogether.
Which meant we were a good two and a half
miles away from the swamp. I scoured the area
for some sort of vehicle. A forklift or a tractor or
something. But no luck.

"It's no use," I said. "We're going to have
to walk." Moonbeams still glimmered through
the treetops, but the melodic garble of a drowsy
magpie told me sunrise would only be an hour or
two away. Jumpy and the other frogs leapfrogged
playfully and babbled contentedly about freedom
and the comforts of home. They were the happiest

bunch of amphibians I'd ever seen. And the slowest. "Hurry up," I said as they flopped along behind me. "Hop faster! I need to get home before my parents wake up."

When we finally slithered down the bank into the swamp, the frogs' triumphant croaks vibrated through the wetland. And as word spread about their return, the excited squeaks, clicks, and calls of a hundred swamp animals added to their merry song.

"Woo-hoo!" hooted the owl. "The frogs are saved."

"Yippee," hissed the tiger snake. "Froggy sssnacks are back on the menu."

"Ka ka ka kaa!" cheered the kookaburra. "The mosquitoes have been driving me ka ka ka kaa."

"Buzzzzzz off!" whined the mosquitoes.

Rising onto his hind legs, Jumpy addressed the gathering crowd with a sweep of his front

foot. "Vertebrates and Invertebrates," he declared. "Darcy Moon, our Earth Guardian, has succeeded!" The swamp animals hustled and bustled for a better view. "The evil Sid Bellows captured these good frogs," continued Jumpy. "He locked them up and harvested their breathing mucus."

The animals gasped in shock.

"How awful!"

"But why?"

"It doesn't make sense!"

"Breathing mucus," explained Jumpy, "is
the secret ingredient in Skippity Chips, a food for
humans."

"Nooooo!"

"Terrible!"

"Shocking!"

"But thanks to our Earth Guardian, Darcy Moon," Jumpy continued and all eyes turned to me, "the frogs have been rescued! Our home is safe!"

A chorus of cheers erupted.

"Hurray!" croaked the frogs all together. They seized Jumpy and raised him above their heads.

"Hurrah!" cried the galah cockatoos.

"Yesss!" called the tiger snakes.

"Caaarn!" called the crows.

It was chaos. But in a good way. Everyone was shouting, cheering, laughing, and singing. A warm satisfied glow, like the orange glimmer rising from beyond the horizon, seeped through my veins. My job was done. Or so I thought, until a familiar voice sounded sorrowfully over the bedlam.

"It is not yet finished!" said Wizen.

An anxious hush descended over the swamp, and all eyes turned to Wizen.

"What do you mean?" I said. "The frogs are back where they belong."

"And the swamp is full of frog traps," said Wizen. "He will return."

"Holy croak!" shouted Jumpy. "He's right. What do we do?" He stared at me with a desperate look in his eye.

A thousand eager eyes looked my way. The whole swamp was waiting for my answer.

But I didn't have one. All I had was a cold, sinking feeling.

"I have a plan," I said because it sounded better than I haven't got a clue. "But right now we all need some rest. I'll come back tomorrow to fill you in."

"But what if we get caught while you're gone?"

"You won't get caught," I said. "You know

about the traps now. Just keep to the mud and don't go in deep water."

"We can do that," said Jumpy. "And tomorrow you can tell us how to get rid of Sid Bellows once and for all."

"Yes," I mumbled as I turned and squelched away.

But when I finally crawled into my bed, I fell asleep without any idea what to do next.

SNOT FEST

The morning came too quickly. I scratched my
head and stared at my dressing table mirror
in disbelief. My hair was stuck together with
mud and poked in all directions. I looked like a
bewildered sea anemone.

"Darcy?" called Mom. I leaped toward my
bedroom door and pushed it shut before she could
get a decent look at me.

My backside held the door closed while
I flattened my hair down with some spit on the
palm of my hands. "Geez, Mom, can't I get any
privacy?"

"Just letting you know breakfast is ready,"

said Mom through the crack of the door. "It's your favorite. Buckwheat pancakes!"

"Okay, okay! I'll be there in a minute." I waited until I heard the clinking of cutlery back in the kitchen, then ran to the bathroom, showered the mud off my body, and scraped a comb through my hair. Despite everything, I was keen to eat. Especially pancakes! All that swamp air had left me famished. Ten minutes later I was dressed, ready for school, and scarfing down my breakfast.

"I'm sorry about barging in on you this morning," said Mom as she pulled her chair close and gazed at me lovingly. "Your inner goddess is blossoming," she said with a dreamy smile. "Your abundant spirit needs space."

"Who needs space?" called Dad from the back door as he kicked off his rubber boots and began washing his hands in the sink.

"Darcy does," said Mom. "She's blossoming."

"Blossoming, hey?" Dad sat down opposite, smothered his pancakes with maple syrup, and picked up the school newsletter. "Sounds like hard work," he said as he skimmed the front page.

"I am NOT blossoming!" I said. "Do I look like a jacaranda tree to you?"

"More like a spinifex bush," said Dad pointing at my hair with his fork.

"Funny." I scowled. "Not!"

"Speaking of trees," he said, tapping his finger on an article in the school newsletter. "It's Save-a-Species Day next week." My stomach did a flip-flop. I was suddenly in the canteen again, holding my empty chip bag with Michael clanking the donation can in my face. "Aaaaaand," Dad continued nervously, "your mom and I were hoping we could volunteer to plant a few saplings."

They both looked at me with beseeching possum eyes. I couldn't believe it. They were actually asking permission to be seen with me.

"I promise I'll wear a bra," said Mom.

"And I'll use deodorant," said Dad.

I groaned and let my head fall onto the table with a thud. Could things get any worse? I was a terrible daughter and a hopeless Earth Guardian.

Mom placed her hand on my back. "Are we really that embarrassing?" she said.

"It's not that," I whispered into the tablecloth.

"What is it then?"

"I spent the Save-a-Species money," I said.

There was a long silence. "You what?" said Mom eventually.

"I spent the money."

"You spent the donation money?"

"Yes."

"The donation money for Save-a-Species Day?"

"Yes."

"I don't understand," said Dad. "What did you spend it on?"

"Skippity Chips," I said.

"You spent the Save-a-Species money on Skippity Chips?"

"Yes."

"Skippity Chips?"

"Yes."

"I don't understand," said Mom. "What are Skippity Chips?"

I groaned and lifted my head just far enough to bang it back down on the table again. Thump. "Potato chips," I said.

"Potato chips?" said Mom.

I couldn't stand it anymore. The swamp was dying, and my parents were repeating everything I said. "All the kids buy them even though they're disgusting." My eyes filled with tears and my breath caught in my chest. "I didn't want to be left out," I sniffed.

"Are they the chips Sid Bellows invented?" said Dad.

I slowly lifted my head off the table and looked at him. "What?" I said wiping some snot from my nose with the back of my hand. "How did you know that?"

Dad waved the school newsletter in his hands. "It's in here," he said. "Apparently he's the guest of honor at your assembly today."

I groaned, smacked my forehead on the table

for a third time, and blinked miserably into the tablecloth. "I forgot about that," I said.

"He's a millionaire," said Dad. "You should ask him to donate to Save-a-Species." I could hear the excitement in Dad's voice. "It's perfect! You'll make up for spending your donation money. And this Sid Bellows," said Dad, pointing to the article with his finger, "can make some good press by helping the environment."

I thought of all the frogs, scared to go in the water in case they got captured again. "I don't

think he cares much about the environment," I said, holding back the tears as best I could.

"Of course he does," said Dad. "Remind him about the endangered tortoises."

What could I say? I pulled a tissue from the box on the table and blew my nose. Of course, the tissue wasn't strong enough, and a big bubble of snot burst all over my hands.

"Oh dear, your emotions are all out of whack." Mom handed me a handkerchief. "Stay home today and realign your energies."

It was tempting. But hiding at home didn't sound like much of a plan. Then again, what could going to the assembly achieve? I mean, even if I stood up and told the whole story, Sid would just deny it. No one would believe me without proof. And I didn't have any. All I had was a bunch of talking animals and . . .

That was it!

I wiped my hands on my school skirt

and pushed my hair behind my ears. "Maybe Dad's right," I said, standing up from the table decisively. "Perhaps the assembly is the perfect opportunity to set things right."

"Good for you," said Dad. "You go get 'em."

"Does this mean we can help out at Save-a-Species Day?" said Mom.

"Of course you can," I said. "I'm sorry for being such a numbskull."

"You're not a numbskull," said Mom, wrapping her arms around me. "You're a child of life. Seeking your path. Finding your way." She nuzzled my hair with sticky maple syrup lips.

"All right, all right." I slipped from her grasp and skidded toward my schoolbag. I had no time to lose. The assembly would start straight after lunch, and if my plan was going to work, I had a lot to do at the swamp first. "I'll work really hard for Save-a-Species Day," I said as I grabbed my bike helmet from the hat stand and buckled it under my chin. "I'll push wheelbarrows, pull out weeds, pick up litter. You'll see. I'll make up that five bucks with hard work and sweat."

"That's right, Darcy," said Dad. "The Moon family will do our bit. My digging will add at least another twenty bucks. And did your mom tell you about her wonderful idea?"

Mom grabbed her panpipes from the buffet and clutched them to her chest. "I've been taking lessons specially!" She beamed. "I'll create a musical bubble of peace and love to soothe the baby trees through their stressful ordeal."

Dad's cheeks were ruddy with delight. "You see?" he said. "Priceless!"

I took a deep breath. Oh well, I thought. At least she'd be wearing a bra.

A SPECIAL GUEST

"Settle down, children," announced
Mr. Bainbridge at assembly. "As you all know,"
he continued, "we have a very special guest
talking to us today."

"I can't believe he came," whispered Taylor
to one of her friends. They were sitting cross-
legged in front of Jedda and me, which was good
because we could slouch down and hide behind
their ponytails.

"Where were you this morning?" asked
Jedda.

"I'm a child of life," I explained. "I was
finding my path."

"Right," said Jedda, and quickly changed the subject. "Doesn't this guy have anything better to do than chat with a bunch of scabby schoolkids?"

"Shhh." I put a finger to my lips and pointed to the front.

Mr. Bainbridge had his hand cupped to his ear. It was his secret assembly sign and meant *You're carrying on like a bunch of chimpanzees. Be quiet NOW!* He waited a few seconds while everyone stopped fidgeting, then continued. "Our guest was a student at Quagmire Primary many years ago," he said. "Since then, he has invented Quagmire's newest and most popular snack, Skippity Chips, led the fastest-growing business in Australian history, and become one of Australia's richest men. He is one of our biggest success stories, and it is a great pleasure to welcome back Mr. Sid Bellows!"

Applause rang out through the hall area.

"Thank you for your warm welcome," said Sid. "I know you all want to hear about what it's like to be me, so . . ." He went on and on, talking about cars and money and meeting the mayor, but I was too nervous to listen much. It was like the sound was turned down.

"Does anyone have a question for Mr. Bellows?" said Mr. Bainbridge.

Taylor's hand shot straight up.

"Taylor," said Mr. Bainbridge.

"We would all like to know," said Taylor with a flick of her hair, "whether the supply of Skippity Chips will be affected by the factory fire we read about in the newspaper this morning?" Mumbles and mutters of agreement swept across the assembly as she sat down.

"Very good question," said Sid. "But the fire was small. A minor setback. Production will be resumed within a couple of days." The assembly released a sigh of relief.

"Gribbit." A tiny croak drifted down from the beams above. Finally! My signal. I threw my hand in the air and wiggled and squirmed so Mr. Bainbridge knew I had the most important question in the room.

"Darcy Moon," said Mr. Bainbridge. I stood up and pulled my undies out of my bum. I always thought better without a wedgie.

"Ahem." I cleared my throat and bowed dramatically. Sid pretended he didn't recognize me, but I could tell he did because his eyes narrowed and his puffy red cheeks started to quiver. I knew what to do, though. I had a plan, and if it didn't work, nothing would. "I was wondering" — I spoke loud and extra slow so everyone could hear, even up the back — "what goes on in that factory? The one where the fire was?"

Sid cracked his neck deliberately to the side. "That factory is where we produce our famous Skippity Chip flavor."

"And what flavor is that?"

"Skippity Chips," he said in a well-rehearsed voice, "are flavored with all natural ingredients."

"Can you tell us what natural ingredients are they, exactly?"

I didn't really expect him to tell the truth. But boy, it felt good to see him squirm! His ears turned purple, and his right eyebrow twitched like a convulsing caterpillar. "That," he said, "is a trade secret."

"But I'm a vegetarian," I said, "and I wouldn't want to eat them if they were flavored with chicken for example . . . or frogs or . . ."

"Darcy Moon!" interrupted Mr. Bainbridge. "Remember your manners!"

"But the label isn't clear," I said. "What if the chips *were* flavored with frogs? Wouldn't you want to know?"

"They are not flavored with frogs, Darcy."

"But what if they were?"

"Darcy Moon!" snapped Mr. Bainbridge. "What has got into you? Why are you asking?"

I took a breath and looked upward. "Well," I said, pointing to the rafters above. "I just wondered, if Skippity Chips aren't flavored with frogs, what are *they* all doing here?"

Everyone looked up, and a sea of shiny eyes blinked down. I had no idea what would happen next. But I knew one thing: people might not believe me, but they couldn't ignore an assembly full of frogs.

"What the — ?" said Mr. Bainbridge, but before anyone had time to think, there was a whooshing noise, an explosion of croaks, and a deluge of green frogs rained down all around us.

They were everywhere. Flying through the air, leaping from kid to kid, croaking excitedly and hurtling about like tiny acrobats in a crazy green circus. They aimed straight for people's faces. One swung from Mr. Bainbridge's earlobe and another stuck a gluey red tongue up Michael's nostril. Yet another landed *splat* on Taylor's head and got tangled in her ponytail.

"Aaaaaaaah!" She slapped at her head and jumped onto Mr. Bainbridge's shoulders. "Help me!" she squealed, kicking her legs like a hysterical octopus.

Jumpy crowd-surfed past me and gave the thumbs-up. Our plan was working perfectly.

"Get off!" shouted Mr. Bainbridge, spinning around, trying to shake Taylor from his back. "What's going on?"

Sid dropped to all fours. He grabbed at frogs and stuffed them into his trouser pockets. "Don't let them get away!" he shouted. "Don't let them get away!" He lunged after a frog with chunky leg muscles, but it hurdled sideways, and Sid flopped onto the floor with a *thud*. "Blow this!" he mumbled, heaving himself to his feet and pulling a handful of bills from his back pocket.

He waved his fist in the air. "Anyone who catches a frog gets a dollar!" he announced.

Well, that was it. Kids were running in every direction, jumping, sliding, and tackling frogs. Frogs skidded between ankles and knees and slipped through grubby fingers. "Here froggy, froggy, froggy," cooed Michael sprinkling Tic Tacs on the floor in front of him. "Come here, froggy. There's a good froggy."

It didn't take long for Sid to run out of dollars. He pulled out a wad of cash and started paying five, ten, even twenty bucks a frog. His trousers were squirming and frogs were jumping out of his shirt collar as quickly as he shoved them in. "I'll give a hundred bucks for a container big enough to fit them all," he announced and there was a mad rush toward the garbage cans.

"You can't put them in there!" Jedda's voice cracked as she shouted to the crowd. She screwed up her face and kicked the bin hard onto its side.

Frogs spilled, blinking dizzily, onto the concrete. Jedda stood over them with her arms outstretched protectively.

Mr. Bainbridge finally shook Taylor off his back. He put two fingers in his mouth and whistled, but no one took any notice. "Calm down, children!" he called and clapped three times. "Hands on heads!" A few nervous-looking kids did what they were told, but no one else seemed to hear. With every bill that left Sid's pocket, the crowd got wilder. Taylor's mouth gaped open so wide I could see her taste buds drying out like toad warts in the breeze. Frogs dodged and weaved while kids charged this way and that, bumping into each other, cheering, skidding, and crashing to the floor.

Then something really weird happened.

Mr. Bainbridge lost it.

"QUIEEEEEEEEEEEEET!" he bellowed, which doesn't sound that weird, except purple veins popped out on his forehead and the dangly thing at the back of his throat got blasted halfway out his mouth. Which was definitely very weird (and pretty gross too), but it did seem to work. The crowd took one look, and the frenzy began to quiet down.

"The show is OVER!" yelled Mr. Bainbridge. "It's time to return to class."

"But something is wrong!" cried Jedda as the crowd slowly shuffled past her toward the exit. She cradled a tiny frog and stroked its cheek. "Why are they so far from home?"

"Don't worry, Jedda," said Mr. Bainbridge. "I'll call the wildlife people as soon as everyone is back in class."

I looked around for Jumpy and spotted him squirming out of Sid's shirt collar. He flashed me a triumphant grin and lifted his webbed fingers in a victory sign. We both knew the wildlife people couldn't miss Sid's frog traps once they got to the

swamp. Not after we'd stacked them up in the parking lot this morning and painted "Property of Sid Bellows" all over them.

"What wildlife people?" shrieked Sid.

But Jedda nodded, satisfied. "Good idea," she said. "My dad told me they're always catching animals at Aroona. For tagging and weighing. They'll know what to do."

"For the love of money, we don't need any wildlife people!" shouted Sid. "We can catch these frogs ourselves!" He looked about to see if anyone was interested. "Don't you get it?" urged Sid. "I want the frogs, and I'm prepared to pay for them!"

"Ahem!" coughed Mr. Bainbridge. "No disrespect, Mr. Bellows," he said through clenched teeth, "but you are not helping the situation."

"Don't be so uptight, Bainbridge," said Sid. "Everyone's got a price. What's yours? A thousand? Two thousand?" He counted out a bunch of notes. "What's it going to take?"

I stomped my foot on the floor. I couldn't stand it any longer. "Don't you understand?"

I glared at Sid. "Some things just can't be bought!"

"You again!" said Sid, his voice quivering with frustration and rage. "Don't you ever give up?"

"You can't buy a swamp full of frogs!"

"Why not?" said Sid. "They're no good to anyone else." He grabbed a passing frog and gripped it so hard its eyes bulged. "And besides," he said. "The French have been eating them for years, and no one complains about that!"

"Um . . ." said Mr. Bainbridge looking confused. "What exactly do you want these frogs for, Mr. Bellows?"

"Oh, for the love of money!" exclaimed Sid. "What do you think makes Skippity Chips taste so good? Potato?" Everyone stared, wide-mouthed and stunned. "Frogs!" he hollered, throwing his hands in the air impatiently. "Frogs taste great!"

Silence descended and hung in the air like a confused and nauseous question mark.

"They're not chicken kebab and garlic sauce

then?" said Taylor weakly. She turned pale, slapped a hand over her mouth, and glanced around frantically.

"Look out!" I shouted. But it was too late.

Her eyes wide, Taylor pushed through the crowd, heaving and retching. Vomit spewed through her fingers, spraying in arcs either side of her as she ran. Kids scrambled backward, tripped over feet, and fell into each other.

"Get out of my way!"

"What did he say?"

"Have I eaten frogs?"

"I don't believe it!"

"AAAAAAHHHHHHH!" Mr. Bainbridge waved his arms above his head like electrified eels. "SNAKE!" He pointed to Sid's trouser leg just as a tiger snake disappeared up it.

Sid Bellows scrambled backward and tripped over the microphone cord. "HELP!" He thrashed his legs in the air and kicked his trousers off in

seconds. The snake slithered quietly away, and
Sid promptly fainted in his undies.

"No way!" said Michael. "This is the best
assembly ever!"

TAKE NO PRISONERS

"What on earth just happened?" asked Michael as we tumbled back into class.

"Did he say frogs?"

"In the chips?"

"No way."

"Totally gross!"

"Ew! Ew! Ew!"

Everyone was talking at once.

"Poor little things," said Jedda. "They looked so frightened."

I wanted to tell her they'd loved every minute. But I didn't want to give myself away. So I said things like *Can you believe it?* and *I knoooooow!*

Poor Taylor was still in a complete tizzy. "I hope they arrest that horrible man!" she muttered. Her ponytail was all messed up, and she gulped frantically from a bottle of water.

"Sit down, children!" called Mr. Bainbridge. He had a mobile phone clamped to his right ear and a finger stuffed in his left one. "Frogs!" he said into the phone. "At least a thousand of them . . . very urgent . . . Quagmire Primary . . . thank you . . . see you in ten minutes."

He hung up the phone, slipped it into his back pocket, and cupped his hand over his ear in his secret you're-carrying-on-like-a-bunch-of-chimpanzees assembly sign. Everyone kept carrying on like a bunch of chimpanzees, so he shouted over the top of us. "I'm going to meet the wildlife people now and brief them on what has happened," he said. "Silent reading until I get back."

As soon as the door closed behind him, we

all rushed to the window and peered down the corridor.

People dressed in khaki trousers and black boots were swarming all over the school. They were pulling on plastic gloves and carrying orange boxes toward the undercover area. The distant blare of an ambulance wound its way toward us, then whimpered to a sudden stop out front. Soon after, we saw someone being stretchered out. I could tell it was Sid on account of his huge stomach and flappy underwear.

"Why would they take him to the hospital?" Taylor asked.

"In case he got bitten by that snake," explained Jedda. "They're deadly, you know!"

"Good!" said Taylor, which really wasn't like her because she was usually such a caring person.

Back in the corridor an important-looking woman was talking to Mr. Bainbridge. She wore the same khaki pants and boots as the others, but she had dangly parrot earrings and a notepad and pen. She kept nodding and writing things down. Then the school principal, Ms. Mueller, turned up, and the three of them stood together with their eyes all squinty and serious until someone must've made a joke or something because they went all relaxed and smiley with each other. Then, just like that, they shook hands and Mr. Bainbridge strode back toward the classroom.

There was a mad rush to get back to our seats and open our books. Mr. Bainbridge burst into the room just as several kids skidded into their chairs. I fumbled my silent reading book and sent it flying into the ceiling fan. Luckily, Mr. Bainbridge didn't seem to mind. Or even notice.

"I won't keep you in suspense," he said, ignoring the pages of my book as they fluttered to the floor. "Mr. Bellows has been taken to hospital for observation, but a snake bite has been ruled out."

"I feel sorry for the snake," said Taylor.

"The snake has been captured, humanely of course," said Mr. Bainbridge.

"And the frogs?" asked Michael.

"Are they okay?" asked Jedda.

"The wildlife people inform me," said Mr. Bainbridge, "that considering what they've been through, the frogs are extremely healthy. It's almost as if they've enjoyed their little adventure."

"Are you sure?" said Michael. "Even the one that ate a Tic Tac?"

"Yes, Michael, even that one," said Mr. Bainbridge. "They are all perfectly well."

"That's a relief," said Taylor quietly. "It wasn't their fault after all."

"I bet they're ready to go home now,

though," I said. "When will they be released back to the swamp?"

"The majority are being transported there as we speak," said Mr. Bainbridge. "But a few have been kept aside for a classroom activity."

"What?" I jumped up from my seat, my heart racing. "But you can't! They belong in the swamp!"

"I agree with you, Darcy," said Mr. Bainbridge. "But . . ."

"But nothing!" I shouted and banged my fist on the desk. "The food chain needs those frogs!"

"Yes, Darcy. All animals play an integral part in the swamp habitat," said Mr. Bainbridge. "And to reinforce that concept amongst the children, the wildlife people, the principal, and myself have agreed" — he beamed at us and rubbed his hands together excitedly — "that you will be going to Aroona

Park to release the remaining frogs yourselves."

"Oh," I said as I sat slowly back down in my seat.

"So we'll be like real wildlife warriors?" Jedda squealed with excitement.

"All of us?" asked Michael. "You mean we can all help?"

"Yes, all of you," said Mr. Bainbridge. "So hurry," he ordered with a grin. "There's a bus waiting out front for us now."

FAREWELL

Before we knew what was happening, the bus had arrived at Aroona Park. Prodding and shuffling the other kids down the steep steps, I crunched out onto the gravel and looked around. I'd never seen the place so busy. Apart from the busload of kids spilling into the parking lot, there were wildlife people scattered all over and a crowd sheltered under a makeshift shade tent. There was even a television news crew setting up by the edge of the swamp. So many people! And all here for the frogs!

"Everyone in a line behind Taylor," called Mr. Bainbridge. He hovered one hand above

Taylor's head and motioned his other arm in the direction he wanted us to line up. "Single file," he said.

"This is so cool," said Michael, slipping in front of Jedda and me. "Way better than math!"

"Yeah!" said Jedda. "This sort of stuff never happens. I feel like Bindi Irwin."

"Collect your frogs from the tent," announced Mr. Bainbridge. "Then make your way to the news crew to await further instructions."

We all shuffled along. "How did you figure it out, Darcy?" said Taylor. "About the frogs, I mean."

I shrugged. "My parents are pretty into nature and stuff," I said. "Maybe I'm a chip off the old block."

"Ha!" Michael laughed. "Good one, Mooney."

"Well, however you did it," said Taylor, "it was brilliant."

"I agree," said Michael. "I've never had this much fun at school — ever!"

"Do you think we'll be on TV?" said Jedda, pointing to the TV crew.

"Looks like it," I said. "Can I come watch at your house?"

"Sure," said Jedda. "Would you guys like to come too?"

Taylor and Michael both nodded excitedly.

"What a lovely idea!" said Taylor.

"I'll bring the chips," said Michael with a wink. "Salt and vinegar flavor."

We all laughed and grinned at each other.

"That sounds great," I said.

We filed eagerly through the tent and past a trestle table stacked with small plastic aquariums. They had green lids full of air vents, and inside each one was a tray of water and a frog.

Taylor was first in line, so she got hers first. "Don't worry, little froggy," she cooed through the air holes as she wandered toward the news crew by the swamp. "That horrid man can't hurt you anymore."

Michael patted the side of his aquarium with his finger. "I've always loved frogs!" he said. "They're so cool!"

"You'll be home soon," said Jedda, cradling hers protectively. "It's nearly over now."

Then it was my turn, and all I could do was stare in complete and utter amazement. Inside my container, sitting casually on his back legs and puffing on his air sac like he did this sort of thing every day, was Jumpy! He winked up at me and grinned.

"G'day, kid," he galumphed. "Looks like we did it."

"Shhhhh," I whispered, glancing about. "Someone might hear us."

"What if they did?" he said, nodding at the kids meandering all around us. "Seems like talking to frogs is the new cool thing."

And he was right! Absolutely everyone was laughing and chatting away to a frog. Like it was a totally regular thing to do. "Well what do you know?" I giggled. "I must be the coolest person on earth."

It was all too much. My insides were bursting with triumph and glee. "We did it!" I blurted. "We saved the swamp! We saved the swamp! We saved the swamp! We . . ."

"We sure did!" said Jumpy, pointing a webbed toe toward the pile of cages we'd planted earlier. A group of wildlife people hovered around them, taking photos and placing bits of evidence into plastic bags. "And this time," he said. "Sid Bellows won't be coming back." He blinked up at me with his eyes all quivery and earnest. "We'd be chips without you, Darcy," he said. "Thanks."

"Everyone this way," called Mr. Bainbridge, waving his arms above his head from beside the swamp. "This is Geeta Green," he said,

introducing the dangly-parrot-earring lady.
She gave us a hello salute. "Ms. Green is the
coordinator of today's release exercise," said
Mr. Bainbridge. "Please listen closely to her
instructions."

"Good afternoon, children," said Ms. Green.

"Good afternoon, Ms. Green," we all
chorused back.

"What you need to do," she instructed, "is
get yourselves into a row at the water's edge."
She pointed down the bank to the shallows below
where a cameraman stood knee-deep in the
swampy water. "The TV crew will be filming the
whole thing for the Skippity Chip story tonight.
So we want lots of smiles. And make sure your
frogs are in clear view. When you're in position,
wait for the cameraman to say when, then lift
the lid and place your cage on its side next to
the water. The frogs will hop out unassisted.
And you" — she spread her arms out — "will

have helped restore balance to our precious swampland."

Michael elbowed me in the ribs. "And we'll be famous!"

"Come on kids," called Mr. Bainbridge, who had already climbed down the bank. "Careful where you step."

I gripped the aquarium tightly under my arm and clambered down the slope. One by one the others followed, and soon everyone had dropped, slipped, skidded, or scooped their way into the mud and were nudging along the edge of the swamp.

"A bit to your left . . . that's it . . . closer together . . . beautiful . . ." said the cameraman as we jostled into position side by side. "Now everyone crouch down and place your containers on the ground in front of you," he said, hoisting his camera onto his shoulder and peering through the lens. "Looking good, kids. I'll count down from five. Open your lid when I get to zero. Are you ready? Here we go. Five . . . four . . ."

An ancient echo, like a vibrating gong, suddenly resounded in my ears. I glanced about in alarm, but no one else seemed to hear it. Michael, Jedda, Taylor, and the others stayed crouched, silent and still, waiting for the instruction to open their lids.

"Earth Guardian, Darcy Moon!" resonated the sound. It was Wizen. But where was he?

". . . three . . ."

I looked around hurriedly but couldn't see him anywhere.

"On the log," croaked Jumpy. I scanned around, and there, floating serenely past on a decaying log, was Wizen. He stood taller and stronger than I'd ever seen him before. His head held sturdy and proud toward the treetops. "Be quiet and listen," whispered Jumpy.

Wizen's inky eyes shone directly into mine.

His words sounded in my head like we were psychic. "On behalf of us all, I am here to thank you . . ." he said.

I willed with my eyes for him to hear my thoughts too. *There's no need to thank me. I should be thanking you — for believing in me.*

"Thank you for helping in our time of need," said Wizen. "For returning balance to our home."

". . . two . . . one . . ."

"When the last frog is released, you will hear us no longer. Your job will be completed."

But it isn't a job. You are my friends!

Wizen turned his gaze from mine. "Listen well and be ready, Earth Guardian, Darcy Moon. For whenever and wherever danger lurks, your friendship will be called upon again."

I hardly knew what to think. I looked to Jumpy for an answer, but he just gave me a watery-eyed wink. "So long, kiddo," he galumphed. "It's been a blast."

". . . Zero!" called the cameraman. "Release your frogs!"

Together we clicked open the lids and watched, wordlessly, as one by one the frogs hopped lazily to their freedom. Flopping shoulder-deep into a puddle, Jumpy paused long enough to fill his throat sac with fresh swampy air. Then, with one powerful kick of his legs, he disappeared under the surface and was gone. The chant of a cicada's song hummed in the air all around, its volume rose slightly and there was a rush of wind as a flock of black cockatoos screeched past overhead.

And then Jedda shouted, "LOOK!"

"Oh my!" said Ms Green. "It's a Western Swamp Tortoise!"

"No way!' said Michael. "Is that the dude that's endangered?"

"It sure is," said Ms Green. "You are very privileged, children. Take a long look. These creatures are usually very shy."

The cameraman shook his head like he

couldn't believe his luck. "This is brilliant footage!" he said, adjusting himself in the mud to get a better angle. Wizen paddled toward the lens, his webbed toenails scraping the log either side of his scaly shell. "It's almost like he's trying to tell us something."

"He's saying thanks," I said. "Thanks for bringing the frogs home."

Wizen turned to catch my gaze one last time, then dove into the murky depths below.

SAVE-A-SPECIES DAY

"Do I smell all right?" Dad knuckled me on the head and pushed his armpit into my face as we walked toward the swamp for Save-a-Species Day.

"Daaad! Stop doing that." I screwed up my nose and punched him in the ribs to get away. "You smell fine," I said. Which wasn't actually true. He'd rubbed some of Mom's peppermint oil under his armpits because he couldn't find any deodorant under the sink. A minty whiff seeped out from his T-shirt. But it didn't cover up the compost stuck to his boots and under his fingernails. He smelled like he'd just been to the bathroom to clean his teeth and do a poo.

But I wasn't worried. I mean, he was there. Helping out. And that was more important than smelling good.

I wasn't worried about Mom not wearing a bra either. She had put one on that morning, but by the time we'd squeezed through the hole in the fence and approached the meeting spot by the swamp, she was gasping for air and clutching at her lungs. "I can't breathe," she wheezed, pulling the bra off under her tank top and stuffing it into her bag. She looked at me apologetically. "I've only got little ones anyway," she said. "No one will notice."

"It's okay." I shrugged. And surprisingly, I meant it. I mean, the saplings needed soothing, and Mom had brought her panpipes. What could be better than that?

Most of the kids were there already. Michael, Taylor and the others were all mooching about by the barbecues, waiting to be told what to do. They looked up as we approached.

"Hi Darcy!" called Jedda as we got closer.

"Hi Jedda," I said. "Hi everyone. This is my mom and dad."

"Hi, Mr. and Mrs. Moon," the kids chorused.

"So wonderful to meet you all," said Mom, her armpit hairs shimmering in the sunlight as she blew kisses. "But, please," she said, "call me Harmony."

"And I'm Rocko," said Dad. "Thanks for letting us help save the planet with you."

"I wish my parents would get involved like you guys," said Taylor. "We don't even recycle at my house."

"That's nothing," said Michael. "My dad actually thinks global warming is a good thing!"

"Really?" said Jedda. "How's that?"

"Longer summer holidays," said Michael.

Dad rubbed his whiskers thoughtfully. "Well,"

he said. "I can see his point. But your dad doesn't have to live in the future, does he?"

"No," said Michael, "that's my job."

"Here comes Mr. Bainbridge," said Jedda.

"Hello, class." Mr. Bainbridge strode toward us across the grass. "I've got important news!"

"What news, Mr. Bainbridge?" asked Taylor.

"I've just come from the courthouse," said Mr. Bainbridge, "where Sid Bellows's punishment was handed down. I thought you might like to know what it is."

"Is he going to jail?" asked Taylor, a little too excitedly.

"Better!" said Mr. Bainbridge with a gleeful look in his eye. "He has been ordered to donate ALL his Skippity Chips money to environmental protection charities!"

"Wow!" said Jedda. "That'll buy a lot of saplings."

"It certainly will," said Mr. Bainbridge.

"It's the perfect punishment," I said. "Perhaps now he'll realize there's more to life than money."

"Phoot, phoot, phoot!" Mom blew airily into her panpipes and fluttered around us, her skirt billowing in the breeze.

Mr. Bainbridge gave her a quizzical look. "That's my mom," I explained. "And this is my dad. They've come to help."

Dad stepped up to shake Mr. Bainbridge's hand. "Glad to be of service," he said. "My wife will provide the love. And I" — he flexed a bicep, releasing a mist of minty goodness from his armpit — "will provide the muscle."

"We're grateful to have you," said Mr. Bainbridge. "Now let's get cracking, team. There are spades for those of you digging holes. If you're picking up litter, grab a bag and some gloves. And the rest of you can start unloading the saplings."

There was a flurry of activity as everyone broke into groups.

But I didn't join in right away. I stood still and closed my eyes. I felt the sun on my face and the air in my lungs. The world hummed all around me. Kids laughed, insects buzzed, leaves whispered in the breeze. And loudest of all, but only if you listened right, was the rhythmic chant of a thousand frogs, going busily about their day.

THE END

ACKNOWLEDGEMENTS

I would like to thank: Jeff and Cherie for believing in me; Sian and Thomas for their love and imagination; everyone who read my work and supported me along the way; Fremantle Press for signing me; Cate for her insightful edits; and Michael for the beautiful drawings.

ABOUT THE AUTHOR

Catherine Carvell lives in Singapore with
her husband, children, and two pet turtles.
Sometimes, Catherine talks to the turtles, but
thankfully, they don't talk back.

For more on Catherine go to:

www.catherinecarvell.com